For Megan

First published 2003 by Walker Books Ltd
87 Vauxhall Walk, London SE11 5HJ

2 4 6 8 10 9 7 5 3 1

© 2003 Niamh Sharkey

The right of Niamh Sharkey to be identified
as the author and illustrator of this work has been asserted by
her in accordance with the Copyright, Designs and Patents Act 1988

Sharkey font © 2003 Niamh Sharkey

Printed in China

British Library Cataloguing in Publication Data: a catalogue record
for this book is available from the British Library

ISBN 0-7445-9265-8

The Ravenous Beast

Niamh Sharkey

WALKER BOOKS
AND SUBSIDIARIES
LONDON • BOSTON • SYDNEY

"I AM

THE HUNGRIEST
ANIMAL OF ALL,"

said the Ravenous Beast.
"I'm hungry, hungry, hungry!
I'm so hungry I could eat

the big yellow house on the hill.

Gobble it up! Swallow it down!

Now THAT'S what I call hungry!"

"Nonsense! Smonsense!"

said the little white mouse.
"No one's hungrier than me.
I'm so hungry I could eat

a red boat and a ringing bell.

Nibble nibble! Tuck 'em away!

Now THAT'S what
I call hungry!"

"Hokum!
Pokum!"

said the marmalade cat.
"I'm as hungry as can be.
I'm so hungry I could eat

a bucket, a spade and some red lemonade.

Gnaw 'em! Gulp 'em! Stuff 'em down!

Now THAT'S what
I call hungry!"

"Hooey!
Phooey!"
said the spotty dog.
"No one's hungrier than me.
I'm so hungry I could eat

a roller skate, a birthday cake,
a rubber duck, a ticking clock.

Slurp 'em! Burp 'em! Woof 'em down!
Now THAT'S what
I call hungry!"

"Moo! Moo! Malarkey!" said the black-and-white cow. "I'm as hungry as can be. I'm so hungry I could eat

a castle, a crown, the Queen's dressing-gown, a wellie-boot, all the King's loot.

Munch 'em up! Crunch 'em down!

Now THAT'S what I call hungry!"

"Balderdash! Baloney!"
said the green crocodile.
"No one's hungrier than me.
I'm so hungry I could eat

a suitcase, a wand, a Jack-in-the-box,

a polka-dot sock, a top hat and a spinning top.

Snip 'em up! Snap 'em down!

Now THAT'S what I call

hungry!"

"Flip! Flap-doodle!"
said the grinning lion.
"I'm as hungry as can be.
I'm so hungry I could eat

a ray gun, a rocket,

a humbug from my pocket,

a trampoline, a trombone with a dent,

a bouncing ball, a circus tent.

Bite 'em up! Bolt 'em down!
Now THAT'S
what I call
hungry!"

"Not on your nelly!"

said the big-eared elephant.
"No one's hungrier than me.
I'm so hungry I could eat

an aeroplane, a parachute,

a pot of tea, a hot-air balloon,

a tin of beans, a parcel, a kite and a green bus.

Suck 'em up! Scoff 'em down!

Now THAT'S what
I call hungry!"

"Whoosh! Swoosh!"
said the gigantic whale.
"I'm as hungry as can be.
I'm so hungry I could eat

a pirate's ship, a treasure map,
a piggy bank, a yellow mac, an anchor, a chain,
a flag, a tin drum, yo-ho-ho and a barrel of rum.

Squish 'em in! Squash 'em down!

Now THAT'S what I

call hungry!"

"STOP!"

said the Ravenous Beast.

"I AM the HUNGRIEST of all!

I'm so hungry I'm going to eat

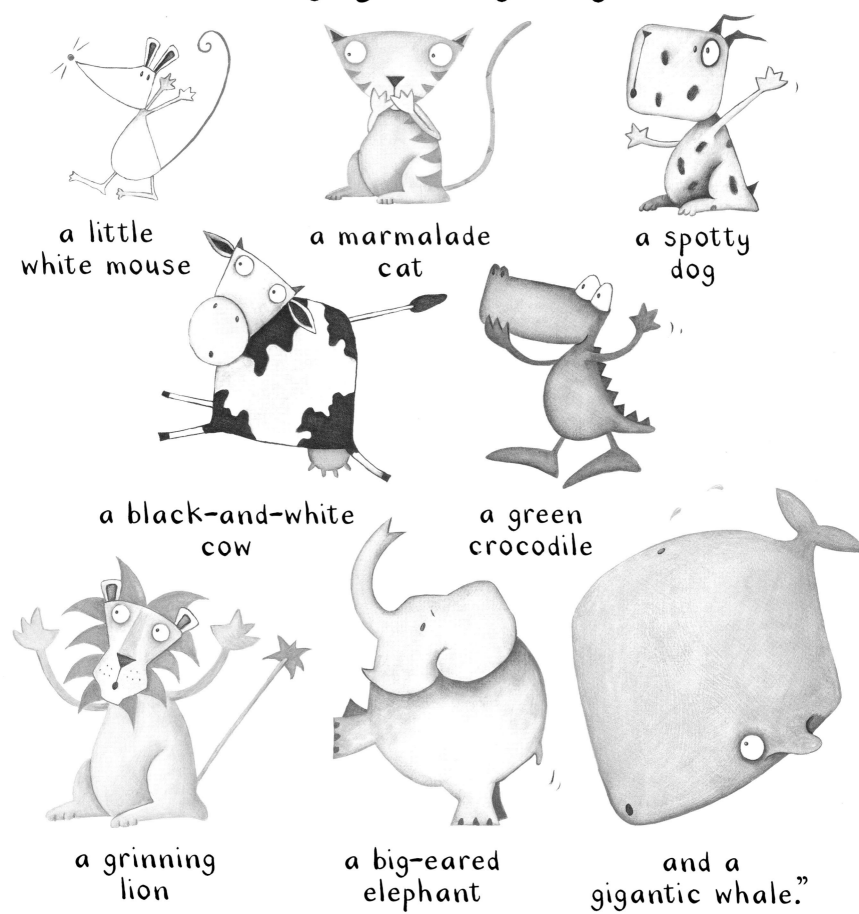

a little
white mouse

a marmalade
cat

a spotty
dog

a black-and-white
cow

a green
crocodile

a grinning
lion

a big-eared
elephant

and a
gigantic whale."

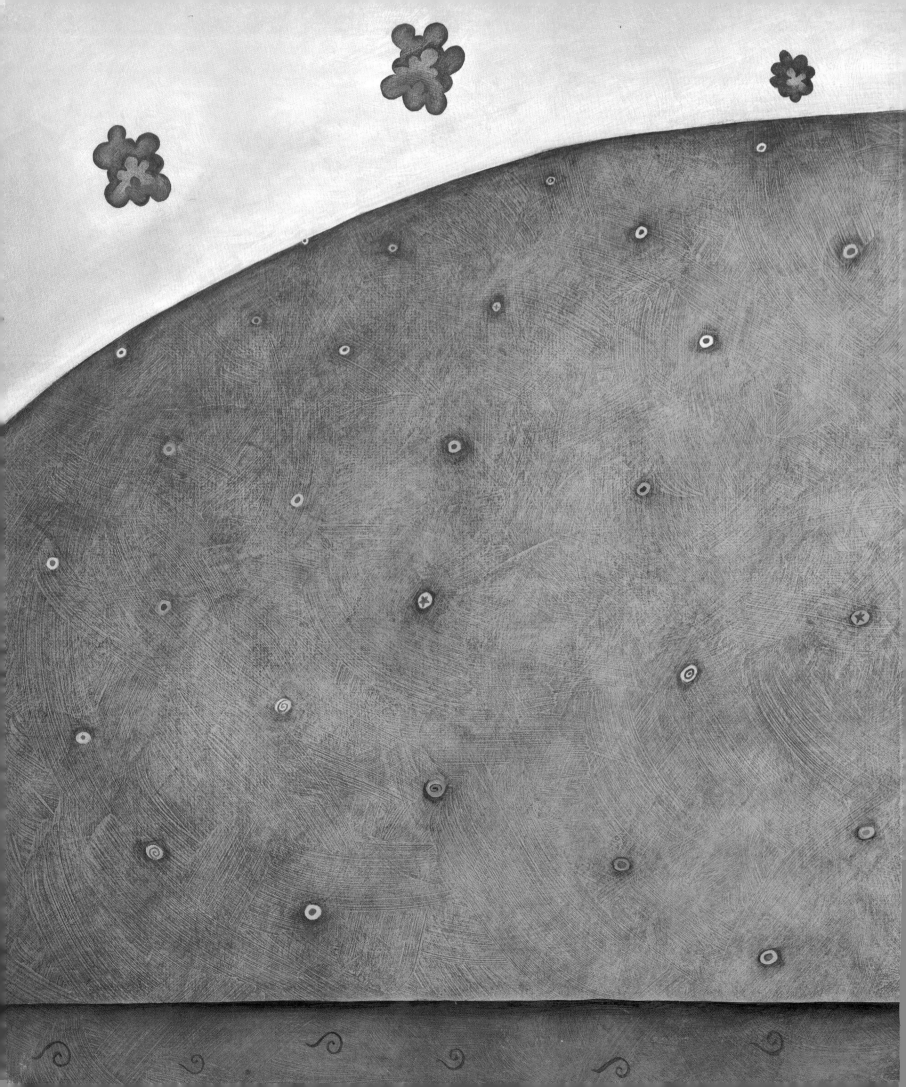